A Deer Named Daisy

written by Rae McSweeney
illustrated by Juli Davis

Balboa Press books may be ordered through booksellers or by contacting:

Balboa Press
A Division of Hay House
1663 Liberty Drive
Bloomington, IN 47403
www.balboapress.com
1 (877) 407-4847

ISBN: 978-1-9822-2356-4 (sc)
ISBN: 978-1-9822-2357-1 (e)

Library of Congress Control Number: 2019902889

Print information available on the last page.

Balboa Press rev. date: 03/13/2019

dedicated to Dr. Watterson

A veterinarian named

Dr. Watterson, practiced in a small town in Oklahoma.

He had a very kind heart. He helped many animals get well when they were sick. He helped heal those that were injured.

One spring day, a local farmer brought an injured baby fawn into Dr. Watterson's clinic. The farmer told the doctor an accident happened when the farmer was harvesting wheat that morning. He explained, "A mother deer built a nest for her new baby fawn in the middle of my wheat field. The fawn was so well hidden at the base of the tall wheat that I did not see her. I accidentally ran over her back legs with my tractor."

"Can you save her?"

Dr. Watterson took one look into the baby fawn's beautiful big eyes, and he knew he had to try to help her. He told the farmer, "I will do the best I can." He made splints for her little broken legs. At first, the fawn didn't know how to walk with her new splints, but soon, she figured out how to hop step with her back legs.

He took the baby fawn home with him, so he could give her the special care she needed. The doctor told her,

"I am going to name you, Daisy."

For many days, Dr. Watterson fed Daisy fresh milk with a bottle and kept her warm by the fireplace in the den. Once Daisy gained back some of her strength, the doctor let her go out into his fenced backyard to get a bit of exercise. People in the neighborhood would see the little fawn in the yard. Neighbors walking by would stop and ask the doctor,

"Why are the deer's legs bound?"

Dr. Watterson would tell everyone Daisy's sad story. He said, "I plan to raise her until her legs completely heal and she can manage on her own." Many of the town's people would stop to watch Daisy's progress and admire her delicate beauty. "What a beautiful sweet fawn. I hope she will be able to walk on her own someday," they would exclaim.

nberdecemberjanuaryfebruarymarchaprilmayjunejulyaugustse

Dr. Watterson also grew
very fond of Daisy.

As the weeks went by, Daisy's legs did heal, and she grew bigger and stronger. She also grew very close to Dr. Watterson. Daisy would follow the doctor wherever he went throughout the house. When he would sit and rest, Daisy would draw up next to him, lay her head on his shoulder, and nestle her nose up against his neck. Dr. Watterson also grew very fond of Daisy. He delighted in taking care of her and watching her grow into a beautiful doe.

When it was time, Dr. Watterson removed the casts from Daisy's legs. Her legs were still a little weak, but the bones had healed nicely. Daisy was expected to make a full recovery. She began staying in Dr. Watterson's backyard where she could move around freely in the more natural outdoor surrounding. There she could receive the exercise she needed to strengthen her muscles.

As the months passed, Daisy grew into an active, elegant doe.

She had the natural need to roam and forage. Daisy began jumping Dr. Watterson's backyard fence to explore the surrounding neighborhood. Time after time, Dr. Watterson would have to retrieve her, and put her safely back into his back yard. Each time he would tell her, "Daisy, you must not jump the fence. You could get hit by a car." But her need to roam was a natural, and she began to get out more frequently.

Dr. Watterson was afraid Daisy would get hurt or possibly shot by a hunter if he kept her at his house where she could jump the fence and wonder off. The Doctor knew what this meant. It was time to find Daisy a permanent home. He knew she needed to live her life in a more natural habitat among other deer. Dr. Watterson called a local wilderness refuge where deer and other animals live in a protected natural environment. He asked them, "Could you take in a young deer and give her refuge in your sanctuary."

The doctor knew Daisy would have a lovely home at the wilderness refuge. They told the doctor, they would be more than happy to take in the young deer. The next week, the doctor loaded her up in his trailer and drove her out to the refuge. The caretaker met them at the gate with a friendly "hello", she said, "You must be Dr. Watterson. We were expecting you."

"Where is little Daisy?"

The doctor led the caretaker to the back of the trailer, opened the door, and let Daisy out. They led her through the gate into the open meadow. Before he untied Daisy from the rope, he hugged her and told her, "I will miss you very much, but you will be happy here among the other deer. They will take good care of you, Daisy."

"You be a good deer." And then he let her go free.

Dr. Watterson walked back to the fence and shut the gate behind him, leaving Daisy standing alone. Daisy hurried back toward the doctor and pushed her nose through the fence. Dr. Watterson touched her nose and said, "You must be brave, Daisy, this is the best place for you to live a happy and natural life of a deer." He walked back to his truck and began to drive away. Tears filled the kind doctor's eyes.

Daisy began making high pitched screaming noises and butting her whole body up against the fence trying disparately to get to the doctor. Over and over, Daisy slammed up against the fence trying to break through. She was hitting the fence so hard the loose wire was cutting her skin and causing her to bleed. Dr. Watterson could no longer stand to see Daisy in this desperate state, so he turned his truck around, got out, and unhooked the gate. He called, "Daisy come here." Daisy came running over to him and nestled her nose up against his neck. He hugged her and said, "We are going home."

Daisy stayed at Dr. Waterson's house for a few more weeks, but she continued to jump the fence and run loose in the neighborhood. The doctor knew something would have to be done about the situation for her safety. A few days later the caretaker at the wilderness refuge called. She said, "Dr. Watterson, we now have several young deer we think Daisy might bond with if you are willing to bring her back out for another visit." Dr. Watterson agreed. The next day he drove her to the refuge.

Indeed, this time when Daisy was let out into the open meadow, she ran to where the young deer were standing near a pond and began to play with them. Dr. Watterson smiled and knew it was going to work out this time. Daisy had a new home. The doctor was very happy, but a little sad at the same time. He told the caretaker, "I will miss Daisy very much, but I am very glad she will get to live among other deer in this beautiful protected environment."

Daisy had a new home.

Dr. Watterson called the refuge to inquire about Daisy, regularly. The caretaker would always tell him, "Daisy is getting along well, and she is happy and healthy." One morning about a year later, Dr. Watterson received a call from the caretaker at the refuge. She invited the doctor to come out and told him, "We want you to see how well Daisy is doing." He agreed to come out and see Daisy.

He left the next morning. He pulled up to the refuge's gate where he left Daisy nearly a year earlier. He could see several deer standing by the edge of a grouping of trees. The caretaker came over to greet Dr. Watterson and explained to him why they wanted him to come out to the refuge. She told him, "Daisy has given birth to a baby fawn, and we wanted you to see it for yourself." The caretaker pointed in the direction of the grouping of trees.

Dr. Watterson spotted a beautiful doe with a little baby fawn by her side. It was Daisy.

The doctor wondered, "Will Daisy recognize me after all this time has passed?"

Dr. Watterson called out, "Daisy, Daisy" a couple of times, and waved his hand in the air. Immediately, Daisy's ears went straight up. She turned her head in the doctor's direction and sniffed the air. She then ran toward him at full speed. She stopped right in front of Dr. Watterson, placed her head on his shoulder, and nuzzled her nose into his neck. Indeed, Daisy remembered the Doctor, his kindness, his care, his love. Dr. Watterson wrapped his arms around Daisy and gently stoked her neck.

"My beautiful Daisy girl," he exclaimed.

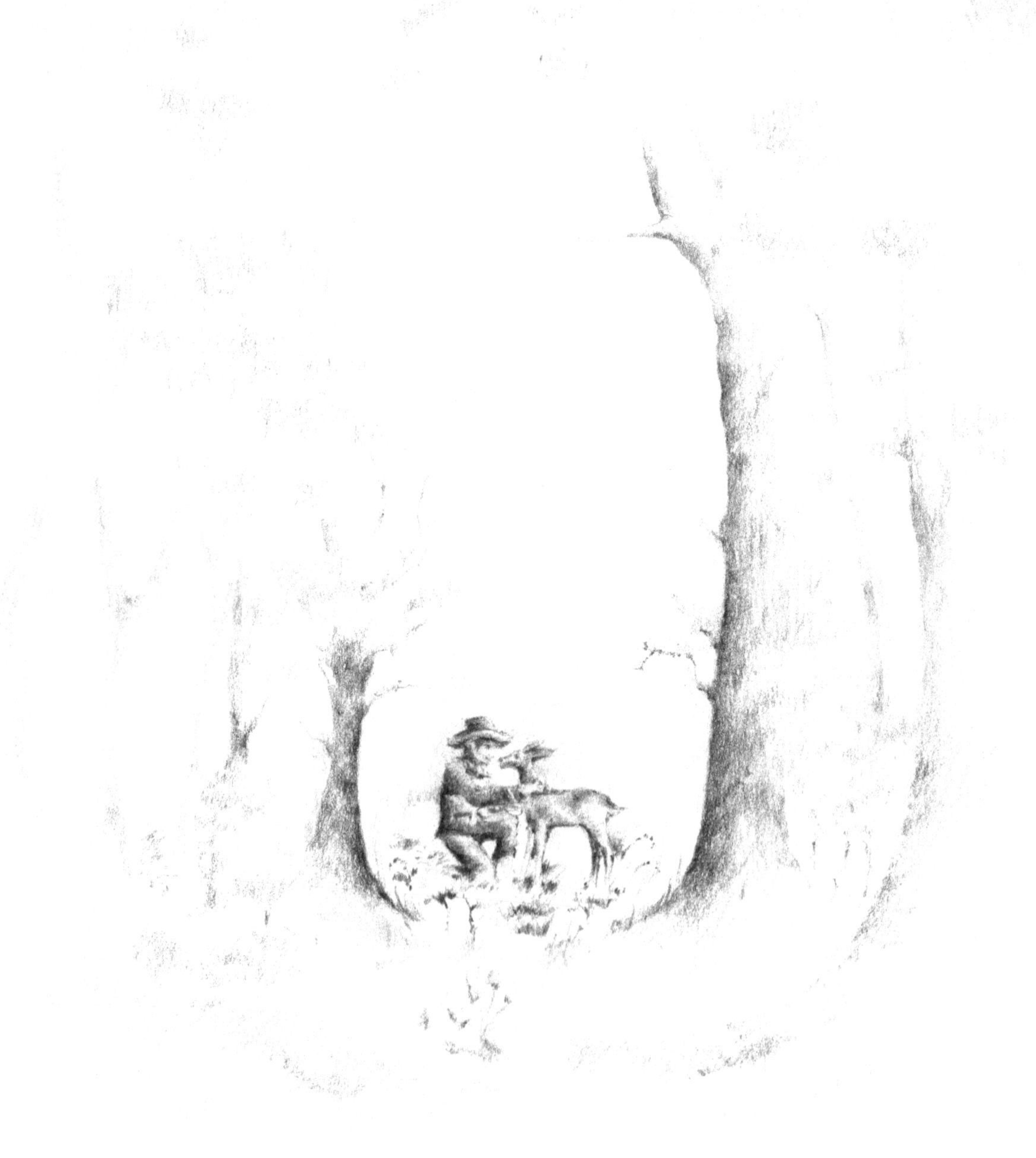

The Doctor looked down at the baby fawn standing next to Daisy. The little fawn looked up at Dr. Watterson with her big beautiful eyes. The Doctor smiled and was reminded of the first day Daisy was brought to his clinic, a helpless little fawn. She was now a strong, healthy doe with a baby of her own. Daisy nudged her baby fawn with her nose and looked up at Dr. Watterson as if to say,

"See my baby. Isn't she lovely?"

"Thank-you, Dr. Watterson. Your kindness and love will carry on."

the author

Rae grew up partially in the small town of Miami, Oklahoma where the story about Daisy takes place. Rae had diverse careers including education, information technology, and nonprofit management. She now lives in Tulsa, Oklahoma with her husband and dog. This is Rae's first book.

the illustrator

Juli Davis is an award winning art director and graphic designer who has worked in the creative industry on a national level, including advertising, fashion retail, corporate communications, and branding. Growing up in northeastern Oklahoma on a generational farm has shaped her style and approach to graphic design, illustration, and interiors-always aspiring to detail and simplicity.

Dr. Watterson holding Daisy

CPSIA information can be obtained
at www.ICGtesting.com
Printed in the USA
BVHW021715050419
544751BV00023B/446/P

9 781982 22356